SIR LANCE-A-LITTLE

and the
MOST ANNOYING FAIRY

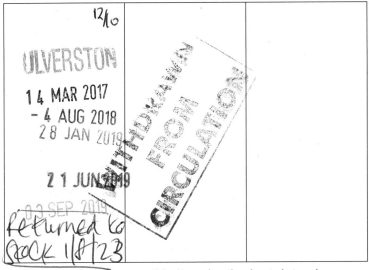

For Sylvie
R.I.

For Finley and Fred
K.M.

ORCHARD BOOKS
First published in Great Britain in 2016 by The Watts Publishing Group

1 3 5 7 9 10 8 6 4 2

Text © Rose Impey 2016

Illustrations © Katharine McEwen 2016

The moral rights of the author and illustrator have been asserted.

A CIP catalogue record for this book is available from the British Library.

ISBN 978 1 40832 522 3 (HB)
ISBN 978 1 40832 528 5 (PB)

Printed in China

FSC
www.fsc.org

MIX
Paper from
responsible sources
FSC® C104740

The paper and board used in this book are made from wood from responsible sources

Orchard Books
An imprint of Hachette Children's Group
Part of The Watts Publishing Group Limited
Carmelite House, 50 Victoria Embankment, London EC4Y 0DZ

An Hachette UK Company
www.hachette.co.uk
www.hachettechildrens.co.uk

and the
MOST
ANNOYING
FAIRY

Rose Impey · Katharine McEwen

ORCHARD

Cast of Characters

Sir Lance-a-Little

Harold the Horse

Princess Plum

Huffalot the Dragon

The Most Annoying Fairy

Sir Lance-a-Little paced up and down outside the dragon's cave. He'd been there *for ages*, waiting to fight his No. 1 enemy.

The dragon had challenged *him* to a fight this time.

ReADY AND
WAITING!
COME
IMMEDIATELY
TO MEET
YOUR FATE!
SIGNED:
HUFFALOT
THE MIGHTY

So Sir Lance-a-Little had come, *immediately*.

But the dragon
still hadn't appeared.
Annoyingly, Sir Lance-a-Little's
cousin, Princess Plum, had
appeared, though. "Did I miss
the fight?" she asked, puffing.

"No!" shouted Sir Lance-a-Little, very loudly, hoping Huffalot would hear. "Because that cowardly dragon won't come out!"

The only reply was a low rumbling noise that sounded like someone groaning, "Go awaayyy." But Sir Lance-a-Little had come to fight and he wasn't going anywhere.

"Coming, ready or not!" he warned the dragon. Holding out his sharp sword, he marched bravely into the mouth of the cave.

But he quickly came out again,
followed by huge gusts of fire.
Much more clearly this time,
they heard the dragon roar,
"I said, go away!"

RRRAGHHHH!

"Maybe he's poorly," Princess
Plum suggested.

"Poorly!" said Sir Lance-a-Little.
"He's a *dragon*!"

But when the dragon finally
appeared he asked, more
sympathetically, "I say, Huffalot,
is something wrong?"

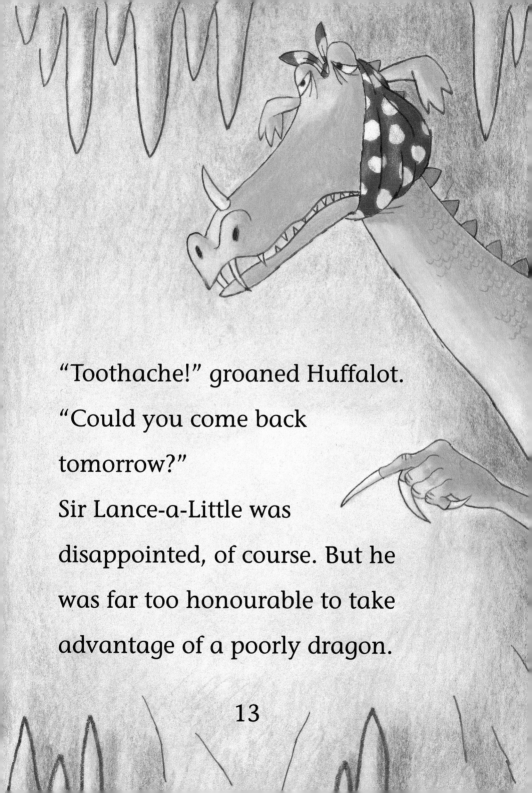

"Toothache!" groaned Huffalot.
"Could you come back
tomorrow?"
Sir Lance-a-Little was
disappointed, of course. But he
was far too honourable to take
advantage of a poorly dragon.

13

He turned and set off home in a
bad mood, with Princess Plum
riding behind him.

"I could fight you," she offered.

But Sir Lance-a-Little ignored her.
Brave knights fought dragons, not
their irritating younger cousins.

On the way home they met a
Most Annoying Fairy.
Sir Lance-a-Little could tell that
she was going to be annoying
because she looked a
lot like his cousin. She
sounded like her, too.

"You can have *three* wishes," the fairy said. "You'll have to be quick, though, I'm in a hurry. And only three, that's the rule, OK?"

But before Sir Lance-a-Little had
time to choose, Princess Plum had
made a first wish.

"I wish I had a suit of armour."

"Princesses don't wear armour!"

the Most Annoying Fairy

pointed out.

"They *might*, if they had any,"
said Princess Plum.

The fairy couldn't really argue
with that. "*Whatever*," she said
grumpily, waving her wand.

Hey presto … There stood Princess Plum, in a full suit of armour, looking very pleased with herself.

Quickly, Sir Lance-a-Little chose
a wish of his own. "I wish I had a
sword—" he began.
"You've got a sword!"
the fairy interrupted.

"*Big enough and sharp enough,*" Sir
Lance-a-Little continued, "*to cut
off a dragon's head with one stroke!*"
Again the fairy grumpily waved
her wand.

20

Hey presto … Sir Lance-a-Little stood there with a huge gleaming sword, much bigger than his own. Now, if only he had someone to fight with it.

Suddenly he knew what else to wish for. But too late …

"I wish I had a sword …" said Princess Plum, "*and* a shield … and a spear … and a lance … and a horse of my own!"

"Just stop right there," said the
fairy. "You know the rules …"

Quickly, Sir Lance-a-Little said, "I wish you'd cure the dragon's toothache."

The fairy waved her wand in the air. *"Whatever!"* she said, grumpily.

Hey presto … When they reached Huffalot's cave, the dragon was waiting for them, looking as fierce, and as cunning, as any dragon in the whole of Notalot. And not at all poorly …

Until he caught sight of Sir Lance-
a-Little's gleaming new sword. It
looked sharp enough, surely, to
cut off a dragon's head with
one stroke.

Suddenly, Huffalot didn't feel at all well. He clutched his stomach and groaned, "Ohhhhh! Ahhhhh!"

"Now what?" Sir Lance-a-Little asked, crossly.

"*Stomach ache*," moaned Huffalot.

"Must be *someone* I've eaten."

And, before Sir Lance-a-Little could stop him, the dragon disappeared into his cave.

The little knight was disappointed, of course, but he was far too honourable to fight a *sickly* dragon. Even one only *pretending* to be sick!

Oh, botheration!

"I'll be back," he shouted into the cave. "Await my challenge!"

And next time he would show
Huffalot, *once and for all*, who was
the bravest and the best.
His name was …
Sir Lance-a-Little!

THE
END

Join the bravest knight in Notalot for all his adventures!

Written by Rose Impey • Illustrated by Katharine McEwen

Orchard Books are available from all good bookshops, or can be ordered from our website:
www.orchardbooks.co.uk
or telephone 01235 400400, or fax 01235 400454.

Prices and availability are subject to change.